Barney Wigglesworth

and the Birthday Surprise

A BOOK ABOUT PERSEVERANCE

Chariot Books
David C. Cook Publishing Co

**Elspeth Campbell Murphy
Illustrated by Yakovetic**

Let us not become weary in doing good, for at the proper time we will reap a harvest if we do not give up. Therefore, as we have opportunity, let us do good to all people, especially to those who belong to the family of believers. (Galatians 6:9, 10, NIV)

DEAR PARENTS AND TEACHERS,

Barney Wigglesworth and the Birthday Surprise is a story illustration of Paul's exhortation to the Galatians.

Most young children are better starters than they are finishers. Partly that's because they have short attention spans—something that's fun becomes boring after a while. Partly it's because they don't know their own limits (they honestly think they can paint the living room), and as a result, bite off more than they can chew.

So kids need help choosing projects that are both reasonable and challenging. And, once a project is under way, they need help seeing it through. Notice that the Epistles don't tell us to "nag one another in the faith." No, the key word is *encourage*. We encourage kids when we let them know that their work is valuable to others, that they're part of the family of believers, and that they're needed. Which is just what Nana McFursoft does for Barney and his friends.

But why mice? It has been said that animal characters are really "kids in fur coats." Children will readily identify with Barney, Gwendolyn, Tillie, and Sam. But because animal characters are one step removed from real life, the concepts of the book come across in a fun, nonlecturing, nonthreatening way.

One final important note: Seeing a project through is not the same thing as perfection. If you have any doubts about this, take a peek at Nana McFursoft's birthday cake! The point is, the mice kids kept their promise and did their best. What more could anyone ask for?

So sit back and enjoy the birthday surprise with your children!

Chariot Books is an imprint of David C. Cook Publishing Co.
David C. Cook Publishing Co., Elgin, Illinois 60120; David C. Cook Publishing Co., Weston, Ontario
BARNEY WIGGLESWORTH AND THE BIRTHDAY SURPRISE
© 1988 by Elspeth Campbell Murphy for text and Yakovetic for illustrations.

Cover design by Dawn Lauck
First Printing, 1988   Printed in Singapore
93 92 91   5 4 3
Library of Congress Cataloging-in-Publication Data
Murphy, Elspeth Campbell.
  Barney Wigglesworth and the birthday surprise. (Little epistles for kids)
  Summary: When the mouse friends encounter difficulties in making a surprise birthday cake for Nana, they consider giving up until Nana offers some good advice.
  [1. Perseverance (Ethics)—Fiction. 2. Mice—Fiction. 3. Baking—Fiction. 4. Christian life—Fiction]
I. Yakovetic, Joe, ill. II. Title. III. Series.
PZ7.M95316Bar 1988   [E]   88-4346
ISBN 1-55513-696-6

The whole crazy cake-baking idea got started when Gwendolyn Scoot, Sam Scurry, and I (Barney Wigglesworth) were over at Tillie Nibbles's house.

Tillie's mouse hole opens right off the church kitchen, and everybody in her family likes to cook.

Tillie's mother was getting ready to make a birthday cake for Nana McFursoft's surprise party.

Mrs. McFursoft is the nicest old lady mouse you'd ever hope to meet. All us kids call her "Nana." That's because she isn't just one mouse's grandmother—it's like she belongs to everyone.

Anyway, Mrs. Nibbles was just getting ready to make Nana's cake, when one of Tillie's little brothers—William—rushed in.

"Mama! Mama! Come quick!" he cried. "Millicent got her tail tangled up in the microphone cord again!"

"That child!" exclaimed Mrs. Nibbles. "How many times have I told her to stay out of the pulpit?"

"Trillions!" said Tillie and William together.

"Oh, dear! Oh, dear!" said their mother. "This could take awhile. How am I ever going to get this cake ready in time?"

"Me, Mama, me!" piped up Tillie. "Let *me* make Nana McFursoft's cake!"

"Don't be silly, Darling," said Mrs. Nibbles. "You've never made a cake all by yourself before."

"But I've helped you trillions and trillions of times," said Tillie. "Besides, I wouldn't be making it all by myself. Gwendolyn, Barney, and Sam will help me."

Mrs. Nibbles didn't look as if that made her feel a whole lot better.

"Oh, please, Mrs. Nibbles! *Pleeeeease*!" said Gwendolyn in her most dramatic voice. "We want to do something nice for Nana!"

"Yes," I said in my most reasonable voice. "And how can you have a birthday party without a birthday cake?"

"Mama, don't worry about a thing!" said Tillie. "You can count on us!"

Sam nodded vigorously.

"All right," said Tillie's mother with a worried smile. "I'm counting on you." And she hurried out after William.

The three of us looked at Tillie.

"NOW WHAT?" asked Sam. (Sam's mouse hole opens right off the choir room. It gets pretty noisy at rehearsals, so Sam has this habit of talking really loud.) "WHEN CAN I LICK THE BOWL?"

"You can't lick the bowl until we mix up the batter," said Tillie.

"Then let us begin!" cried Gwendolyn happily.

But mixing up the batter turned out to be pretty hard work, and soon Gwendolyn was saying, "My arms are positively dropping off!"

"Is the cake almost done yet?" I asked Tillie.

"Not even close," said Tillie, who was beginning to look like she wished she had never even heard of cake. "Now we have to pour the batter in the pan."

That wouldn't have been so bad except we also poured the batter onto the table and the floor and ourselves.

By the time we got the batter in to bake—and the rest of the batter off the floor and the table and ourselves—we were tired and crabby. We went out to sit on the front step.

"I am utterly exhausted!" declared Gwendolyn.

"I wish we'd never started on this," muttered Tillie.

"I don't see why we can't have a birthday party without a birthday cake," I said. "Maybe we should just give up."

Suddenly, Sam said, "SHHHH! QUIET! HERE COMES NANA!"

As soon as Tillie saw Nana McFursoft's kind, old face, she burst out crying.

Nana hurried over and put her arms around her. "Oh, my poor, sweet mouseling! There, there, don't cry. Tell me what's wrong."

Tillie gulped, and when she talked, her voice was shaky from crying.

"We—we were trying to make a birthday cake for—for—someone. And—and it turned out to be *so hard* to do! And we really love the person it's for. But we don't know if we can finish it."

"But what's that wonderful smell?" asked Nana. "Isn't that the cake baking? Well, then! You're halfway there. And you know what I think? I think you don't really want to give up. I think you want to finish your lovely cake—all the way to the frosting. Just imagine how good you'll feel when it's done. You are a good cook, Tillie Nibbles! And you have three good helpers. You just need a little rest. Then you can start again."

So Nana sat with us and told us stories while we waited for the cake to bake and then while we waited for it to cool.

When she left, she shook our paws and said, "Keep up the good work!"

We didn't feel like giving up anymore.
When the cake was ready to frost, we were ready to frost it.

At last we stepped back to look at it.
"BEE-U-TI-FUL!" said Sam.
"Absolutely gorgeous!" breathed Gwendolyn.
"You don't think it's a little lopsided?" asked Tillie.
But you could tell she really thought it was great.
"No, it's just right." I said. "Nana will love it!"

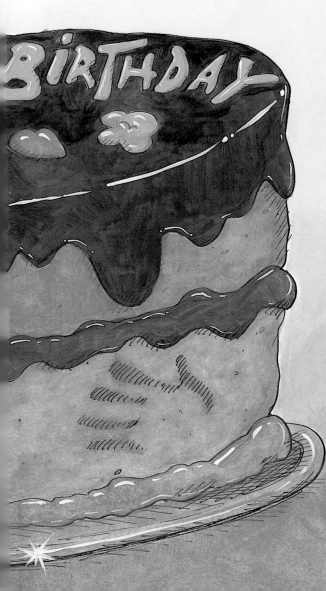

At the party, Nana said to everyone. "Did you see the wonderful, delicious, lovely cake the children made for me?"

And everyone said, "You're kidding! The *kids* made this cake?!"

Tillie beamed and said, "We kept up the good work, didn't we, Nana? And we did it. We really did it!"